kind

princess bitty ★ baby

by Kirby Larson
& Sue Cornelison

★ American Girl®

Special thanks to Dr. Laurie Zelinger, consultant,
child psychologist, and registered play therapist.
Dr. Zelinger reviewed and helped shape the "For Parents"
section, which was written by editorial staff.

Questions or comments? Call 1-800-845-0005,
visit **americangirl.com,** or write to Customer Service,
American Girl, 8400 Fairway Place, Middleton, WI 53562-0497.

Printed in China
13 14 15 16 17 18 19 20 LEO 10 9 8 7 6 5 4 3 2 1

Series Editorial Development: Jennifer Hirsch & Elizabeth Ansfield
Art Direction and Design: Gretchen Becker
Production: Tami Kepler, Judith Lary, Paula Moon, Kristi Tabrizi, Mike Birkrem

Bitty Baby and I picked out our favorite book.

"Daddy," I called. "It's story time."

"First it's get-ready-for-bed time,"
said Daddy. "Do you need help?"

"I can do it myself." I soaped up the
washcloth and rub-a-dubbed my face.
Then I washed Bitty Baby's.

"All clean," I said. "We're ready for story time."

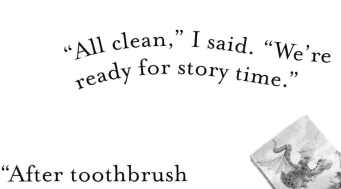

"After toothbrush time," said Daddy. "Do you need help?"

"I can do it myself," I said.

I squeezed out the toothpaste and scrub-a-dubbed my teeth. Then I helped Bitty Baby. Even though she doesn't have teeth.

"Hooray for story time!"
Bitty Baby and I cheered.

"After pajama
time," called
Daddy.

"Daddy's never going to read a bedtime story," I said.

"Can you do it yourself?" asked Bitty Baby.

"No," I said. "I can't read yet."

Daddy peeked in. "Do you need help putting on your pajamas?" he asked.

"I can do it myself," I said.

I dressed Bitty Baby in her
pink-and-white pajamas. I put mine
on, too. "Finally it's story time!" I said.

"Sit here so you can see
the pictures," said Daddy.
We cuddled together on the bed.

"Once upon a time, there was
a clever princess," Daddy began.

I turned the page.

"With a pet dragon," Daddy read.

Bitty Baby loved that part. Me, too.

Daddy kept reading. "The princess was
so clever—"

Ding-a-ling. Ding-a-ling.

"Don't answer the phone!" I said.

"It might be Mommy," said Daddy.

It was Grandma.
Daddy talked...

...and talked

...and talked.

He was never
going to stop.

I stamped my right foot. "I'm tired of waiting for a story!"

Bitty Baby stamped her left foot. "I'm tired of waiting, too."

"Maybe I could *tell* you a story," I said. "Would you like that?"

Bitty Baby nodded. We cuddled on the bed.

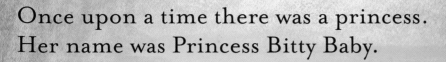

Once upon a time there was a princess. Her name was Princess Bitty Baby.

One day, Princess Bitty Baby found a frog sitting on a rock. A big tear rolled down his frog face. "What's wrong?" asked Princess Bitty Baby.

"A bad witch turned me into a frog," said Frog. "And I can't turn back until someone tells me a story."

Now, Princess Bitty Baby could do many things herself.

She could rake the royal leaves...

...and frost the royal cupcakes.

But she had never told anyone a story before. Frog looked so sad, she decided to try.

"Maybe I could do it," she said.

"Ribbit!" said Frog. That was frog talk for "Hurray!"

Princess Bitty Baby took a deep breath. "Once upon a time—"

"Oh, that's a very good beginning," said Frog, wiping his eyes with a lily pad.

"—there was a dragon,"
Princess Bitty Baby
continued. "The
dragon was in a
bad mood. He
stomped through
the forest and came
upon a little girl."

"'You're in my forest,' the dragon roared. 'I'm going to eat you!'"

Another tear rolled down Frog's face. "The middle of this story seems very sad."

"Don't worry," said Princess Bitty Baby. "There's a happy ending."

Frog sniffled. "I love happy endings."

Princess Bitty Baby went on with her story. "The little girl said, 'I was just going to read a bedtime story. Would you like to listen?'

"The dragon said,
'No one has ever read me
a bedtime story before.'

"The little girl said, 'Sit here
so you can see the pictures.'
The little girl was a very good reader.
And it was a very good story. All about
dragons.

"When she was done, the dragon
said, 'If you read it again,
I promise not to eat you.'"

"Ribbit!" said Frog.
"That's a good promise.
And a good story."

Princess Bitty Baby looked at Frog. He was still a frog.

"I guess it didn't work," Frog said. "Thank you for trying."

"Wait! I almost forgot the most important part," said Princess Bitty Baby. "After that, the little girl and the dragon were friends. The end."

And—*poof!*—Frog turned into…

"Daddy!" I said.

"I'm done with
my phone call,"
said Daddy. "I'm
ready to read."

"I love happy endings, don't you?" I whispered to Bitty Baby.

"And dragons," she whispered back.

For Parents

Make a happy ending

Just like the girl in the story, most young children have limited tolerance for delay and frustration. Fortunately, what they lack in patience, they make up for in their power of imagination. As a parent, you can harness this power to help your little one cope with delays or disappointments.

Fix it in fiction

When something happens that your daughter doesn't like, ask her what she wishes would happen. Then suggest that she tell a story about that very thing happening. For example, if she's becoming impatient waiting for a friend to come over or for the doctor to see her, you could say, "Tell me all the games you and Emma are going to play when she gets here," or "Tell me a story about a little girl who waited *so* long for the doctor to come that when the doctor finally came, the little girl was all grown up!"

Silly solutions work, too

Next time your girl is feeling antsy, try this tack: Ask her, "What if there was a contest to see who could wait the most patiently? Who would win? What would the prize be? What if some of the other kids just couldn't wait—what would they do?" Then sit back and listen as her mind plays out the possibilities. If they are super

silly, so much the better—she'll be happily entertained, and you will, too!

Imaginative empowerment

Your daughter's power of imagination also serves as a learning tool and a stepping-stone to success. In much the same way that athletes imagine winning a competition, children enjoy imagining themselves overcoming problems and accomplishing their goals. This type of creative visualization is a natural way for children to practice success, just as it is for adults. Encourage it.

Build the "patience muscle"

Researchers have found that children who can handle delayed gratification at a younger age are more successful as students many years later. So helping your daughter develop a strong "patience muscle" will not only improve her ability to tolerate frustration and delays, it will also help her be more successful later on in school.

For more parent tips, visit
americangirl.com/BittyParents

curious

loving

confident